WWW.healthhaven

ISBN: 9798820492259

To my family, Dan, Danny, Ryan and Lauren who went on the adventures with me where the stories were born.

Doris
the Happiest Pelican in Aruba

Louise Dougherty

Doris is an awesome pelican who lives in Aruba. She loves to hang out on the rocks in the water with her bird friends.

All day long they catch the breeze, basque in the sunshine, and squawk about the boats passing by giving tube rides.

They watch the people swimming and snorkeling.

Their favorite
activity to watch is
the kids jumping off
the Aruba
dock into the water.
They love
cannonballs and
belly flops.

The bird crew says hi to the tropical fish swimming around the coral reef beneath the rocks and they pop their heads up from the water to say hello.

The birds and the
tropical fish like it
when the tourists
feed them bread and
say hello as they
snorkel by.

Everyday at 2 pm Doris the
pelican leaves her friends on the
rocks by the coral reef to go meet
her favorite tour boat.

Doris flies from the
middle
of the island of
Aruba to the end of
the island near the
lighthouse.

Doris meets the jet ski swimming tour every day for fun and fish. The tour guides, John and Carlos, call her to fly over as they take the families out of the boat to swim with the mini-jet ski.

Doris lands on a mini jet ski as her friends John and Carlos introduce her to the families who are snorkeling.

John and Carlos dive
down to catch some
fish for Doris.

Doris flaps her wings and
shows the crowd how
wide her wingspan is, and
the families cheer. They
love Doris.
Doris is so proud.

John and Carlos
throw the fish and
Doris darts to catch
the fish.
She never misses.

The crowd of swimmers cheered because they had never seen such a smart and friendly pelican.

When Doris is full,
she says goodbye and
flies away.

The families say goodbye and begin to swim by holding on to their mini-jet skis.

Doris flies to the lighthouse house on the tip of the island to settle down for the evening.

She stops at her favorite tree
to say hi to her friends,
the iguanas.

She brings the iguanas
some fruit she saved.
They are always happy
to see her.

They watch the
beautiful sunset
on the beach together.

She loves her life in Aruba
and can't wait to do it again
tomorrow.

Good morning friends.

Made in the USA
Columbia, SC
07 August 2023

21153448R00015